For Miranda Richardson,
with love
F.S.

First published in Great Britain in 1995
First published in Great Britain in this edition 2004
by Orion Children's Books
a division of the Orion Publishing Group Ltd
Orion House
5 Upper St Martin's Lane
London WC2H 9EA

Text © Francesca Simon 1995, 2004
Illustrations © Emily Bolam 2004

The right of Francesca Simon and Emily Bolam
to be identified as the author and illustrator
of this work has been asserted.

Printed and bound in Italy

ISBN 1 84255 109 4

The Topsy-Turvies

Story by Francesca Simon   Pictures by Emily Bolam

Orion
Children's Books

Once upon a time
there lived a family called
the Topsy-Turvies.

The Topsy-Turvies always got up at midnight.

They put on their pyjamas . . .

. . . then went upstairs and had dinner.

'Eat up, Minx,' said Mr Topsy-Turvy.
Minx juggled with the sausages.
'Clever girl!' said Mr Topsy-Turvy.

'Jinx, stop eating with your fork,'
said Mrs Topsy-Turvy.
'You know that's for combing your hair.
Please use your fingers and toes.'

'Could you pass the jam please, Minx?'
said Mr Topsy-Turvy.
Minx dipped her fingers in the jar
and hurled the jam at her father.
'Thanks,' said Mr Topsy-Turvy.

'Could you pass the whipped cream
please, Jinx?' said Mrs Topsy-Turvy.
Jinx flung a handful of cream at
his mother.
'Thanks, dear,' said Mrs Topsy-Turvy.

Then it was time for school.

After school they went to the park.

Then they played beautiful music together

and watched TV.

Afterwards they ate breakfast,

then it was bathtime

and then they all went to bed.

Every night and day
at the **Topsy-Turvies**
was exactly the same

until . . .

. . . one afternoon a loud knocking at the door woke them up.

'Who could that be at this time of day?' yawned Mrs Topsy-Turvy.

It was their neighbour, Mrs Plum.
'Oh dear,' said Mrs Plum. 'Were you just leaving?'
'No,' said Mrs Topsy-Turvy. 'Why would **I** go outside wearing my coat?'

'I'm sorry to bother you,' said Mrs Plum. 'But **I** have to go out.
Could you come over and look after little Lucy? She's as good as gold.'

Mrs Topsy-Turvy was very sleepy, but she liked helping others.
'Of course,' said Mrs Topsy-Turvy. 'We'll be undressed in a minute.'

As soon as everyone was ready, they
went next door to Mrs Plum's house.

'Thank you so much,' said Mrs Plum.
'Do make yourselves at home and have something to eat.'

And off she went.
'Mum, why is Mrs Plum wearing clothes OUTSIDE?' said Minx.
'Shh,' said Mrs **Topsy-Turvy**. 'Everyone's different.'

The Topsy-Turvies goggled at Mrs Plum's house.
Nothing looked right.
'Poor Mrs Plum,' said Mrs Topsy-Turvy.
'Let's make the house lovely for her.'

The Topsy-Turvies went to work.

They fixed, they fussed,

and they put the room in apple-pie order.

'That's better,' said Mr Topsy-Turvy.

'Careful, Lucy, don't put that
apron on, you'll get paint all
over it,' said Mr Topsy-Turvy.

'Lucy! Don't draw on the paper!'
said Mrs Topsy-Turvy. 'Draw on the walls!'
'Isn't she naughty,' said Minx.

'Not everyone can be as well behaved as you, dear,' said Mrs Topsy-Turvy. 'Lucy, what a lovely picture!'

'I'm hungry,' said Jinx.
'So am I,' said Minx.
Mrs Topsy-Turvy looked at the clock. It was almost five.
'We might as well have breakfast,' said Mrs Topsy-Turvy.
'Let's see what food we can find in the bedroom.'

It took them a very long time to find where Mrs Plum kept her food.

'What an odd house,' said Mr Topsy-Turvy.

'How funny to eat in the kitchen,' said Minx.
'Breakfast is under the table,' said Mrs Topsy-Turvy.
'Don't forget to wash your feet.'

'What's for dessert?' said Minx.
'Tomatoes,' said Mr Topsy-Turvy.
'Yippee!' said Jinx.
'But no tomatoes until you finish your cake.'
'Do I have to eat ALL my cake?' said Jinx.
'Yes,' said Mrs Topsy-Turvy.

Suddenly there was a noise at the window. . .

It was a burglar.

'Hurray! We've got
a visitor!' shouted Minx.

'And he's coming through the window!' shouted Jinx.

'Let's make everything lovely for our guest,' said Mrs Topsy-Turvy.
'Please, have something to eat,' said Mr Topsy-Turvy,
throwing tomatoes at the burglar.
The burglar looked unhappy.

'Have some cake!' said Jinx,
hurling his leftovers.

'No, have some of mine!' shouted Minx.

'Mine too!' shouted Lucy.

The frightened burglar escaped as fast as he could.
'Why did he run off?' said Minx.
'I don't know,' said Mrs Topsy-Turvy.

Then Mrs Plum ran in.

'Is everything all right?' said Mrs Plum.

'I just saw a burglar jump out of the window!'

'Everything's fine,' said Mr Topsy-Turvy.
'You chased away a burglar!' said Mrs Plum.
'Thank you so much. Goodness what a mess he made!'
'What mess?' said Mrs Topsy-Turvy.

The Topsy-Turvies waved goodbye and went home.
'Mrs Plum should have said thank you for making
her house so lovely,' said Minx.

'Never mind,' said Mrs Topsy-Turvy.
'It takes all sorts to make a world.'